Josephine

Pleasant Rhymes for Little Readers

Or Jottings for Juveniles

Josephine

Pleasant Rhymes for Little Readers
Or Jottings for Juveniles

ISBN/EAN: 9783337260064

Printed in Europe, USA, Canada, Australia, Japan

Cover: Foto ©Andreas Hilbeck / pixelio.de

More available books at **www.hansebooks.com**

FOR

LITTLE READERS

OR

JOTTINGS FOR JUVENILES

Affectionately Enscribed to the Children of England

By JOSEPHINE

AUTHOR OF "OUR CHILDREN'S PETS."

" Wherever in the world I am,
    In whatsoe'er estate,
I have a fellowship with hearts
    To keep and cultivate,
And a work of lowly love to do
    For the Lord on whom I wait."

MRS. WARING.

LONDON

HOULSTON AND WRIGHT

65, PATERNOSTER ROW

MDCCCLXVI.

LONDON:

J. AND W. RIDER, PRINTERS,

BARTHOLOMEW CLOSE.

PREFACE.

Dear Young Readers,

      To write you a little Volume in simple Verse has been to me a very pleasant task. Many of the Stories it contains are true, and perhaps some of them may not be quite new to you, still, I trust they are interesting enough to bear a second reading.

My desire is to impress upon your young minds the *blessedness of doing good*, not only to the helpless and needy among your fellow-creatures, but also to dumb animals, who have no eloquent voices with which to plead for your pity.

How lovely is the sight of the kind and tender-hearted child, never so happy as when able to aid the poor by little acts of self-denial, and whose delight is to care for the wants of the speechless creatures round him, that repay his unselfish love with grateful affection !

The blessing of Heaven will surely rest upon the head of that kindly child, and he shall grow as the youthful Saviour of old—" in favour with God and man."

Trusting that you will get by heart the lessons of love these pages are intended to teach you, and that you may ever remember—

> " He prayeth best who loveth best
> All things, both great and small ;
> For the dear God, who loveth us,
> He made and loveth all,"—

I am, your affectionate friend,

JOSEPHINE.

The Publishers have much pleasure in stating that a large edition of this Volume, hitherto issued under the title of " Josephine's Jottings," has been exhausted, and a new edition called for. Advantage has been taken of this to alter the title, so as to express more clearly the nature and aim of the Work.

Great pains have been bestowed on the getting up and embellishment of the book, in order to render it still more attractive, and worthy of the acceptance of the "Young Readers," for whose benefit it has been written.

LONDON, *September*, 1866.

CONTENTS.

THE BLACK KITTEN.

LITTLE black pussy stood close by a dish,
Most greedily eating large mouthfuls of fish.
And Margaret she watched her at dinner, and
thought
Her dear, lively kitten ate more than she ought.

But, all in a moment, puss gave a loud moan;
"Oh dear!" exclaimed Margaret, "she's swal-
lowed a bone!"
Her mewing and choking were dreadful to hear;
Poor Margaret was almost afraid to go near.

Her mouth she kept clawing, and then she
rushed round,
Then over and over she rolled on the ground.
"Oh, poor little pussy!" cried Margaret, "if I
Turn coward and leave you, I'm sure you will die!

"I'm certain mamma wouldn't leave *me* alone
If *I* were a kitten, and swallowed a bone!"
So over her pussy her pinafore white
She threw in a moment, and snatched her up tight.

And into the house from the garden she ran,
Exclaiming, "Oh, cook! come as fast as you can!"
And cook she got up to the parlour at last,—
A very fat woman, she couldn't run fast!

She took the poor cat to the kitchen below,
And Margaret went after, and thought her so slow.
She sat in a chair, and she held pussy tight,
And bade little Margaret stand out of the light.

The mouth of the kitten she opened quite wide,
And down in its throat a large bone she espied.
And after some feeling and fumbling about,
The struggle was ended, the bone was got out.

And cook she sat wiping the scratch on her thumb,
And wished there were more that were kind to the dumb;
For God was the Maker of great and of small,
And we should be feeling and good to them all.

Oh, dear little children, be sure that you do
As you would wish others to do unto you!

THE HEAP OF HAY.

WAS little Jenny, and she sat
  Upon a heap of hay,
Beneath the shadow of a tree,
  And read the "Peep of Day."

The blackbird sang his merry song
  Above her curly head,
And hopping boldly at her feet
  Was little robin red.

But Jenny did not care to hear
  The merry blackbird sing,
Nor watched she robin redbreast smooth
  His pretty shining wing.

For, bending o'er her book, she read
  Of Jesus in the sky;
And how the angels come to fetch
  Good children when they die.

The aged gardener, working near,
  Would often look that way,
And wonder why Miss Jenny loved
  Her reading more than play.

At length he close and closer drew,
  And, " Little Miss," said he,
" You have a pretty book—I wish
  You'd read a bit to me."

And little Jenny's eyes of blue
  They sparkled as she said,
" I'll read about the death of Christ,
  And how He left the dead."

" The death of *Christ?*" the gardener asked,
  " First tell me, who was He?"
Said Jenny, " *Don't you know the Lord,*
  Who died for you and me?"

" Ah! Miss, I never went to school,"
  The poor old man replied;
" It seems as if I'd heard His name,
  But nothing else beside."

The tears came into Jenny's eyes—
  " Oh dear! how sad!" she said,
" What! have you not in all your life
  The holy Bible read?

" And did you never go to church
  When you were young?" said she,
" Nor ever say your pretty prayers
  Beside your mother's knee?"

"No; I was never taught at all,"
The aged gardener sighed;
"A single word I could not speak
When both my parents died."

"Oh dear!" said Jenny, "if you like,
I'll come here every day,
And sit beneath this shady tree,
And teach you, if I may.

"Come, sit beside me on the grass,
And let us *now* begin
To read about the Lamb of God,
Who takes away our sin."

With many thanks the gardener sat
The gentle girl beside,
And heard her tell of Jesu's love—
So boundless, deep, and wide.

And when she closed her pretty book,
He scarce a word could speak;
His heart was full of thought, and tears
Were on his withered cheek.

That night, as lost in slumber deep
The aged gardener lay,
He dreamed that holy angels bright
Stood round the heap of hay.

And often as he worked next day,
    Across the field he'd look,
To see if little Jenny kind
    Was coming with her book.

She came at last, that happy child,
    As summer morning bright,
Plucking the king-cups in her way,
    And pink-edged daisies white.

The gardener he had shaken up
    Her soft and fragrant seat,
And swept a pathway through the hay
    For Jenny's tripping feet.

And down again they sat and read,
    And all that summer long
He listened to that pleasant voice,
    As sweet as wild-birds' song.

And when that lovely field was cleared
    Of all the scented hay,
The gardener suffered none to move
    Miss Jenny's heap away.

The sunbeams struggling through the leaves
    That clothed the elm tree tall,
Upon the light locks and the grey,
    Day after day would fall.

But when those leaves so deeply green
  Looked yellow in the sun,
And down upon the grass below
  Came floating one by one—

The aged man and blue-eyed child
  Sat talking there no more,
For stretched upon a bed of pain
  He lay in suffering sore.

And now that dear, attentive girl
  Would seek his darkened room,
With words and deeds of comfort kind,
  To cheer him in the gloom.

And he would talk of God and heaven,
  And Jesus, as he lay,
And how he learned the love of Christ
  Beside the heap of hay.

But weaker every day he grew,
  For he was very old;
And in the churchyard he was laid,
  Before the winter cold.

There, often as she came from school,
  Would little Jenny go,
And leave around the gardener's grave
  Small footprints in the snow.

And oftener still, when spring came back,
   She sought the favourite spot,
And planted on the grassy mound
   The blue forget-me-not.

And thought upon that happy soul,
   Safe in the realms of day,
Who learned of her the way to heaven
   Beside the heap of hay.

THE FROZEN ROBIN.

HE sky was dark, and very loud
   The winter winds did blow,
While Carry at the window stood,
   And watched the driving snow.

And all at once, as soft it fell
   In feathery flakes around,
She spied a little trembling bird
   Upon the frozen ground.

She saw it spread its pretty wings,
   As though it wished to fly;
And then it drooped its head, and seemed
   As if it soon would die!

But oh! to Carry's great surprise,
  It stretched its wings again,
And beat its little scarlet breast
  Against the window-pane.

Then down it fell upon the sill,
  Too weak, alas! to stand;
And Carry gently raised the sash,
  With trembling heart and hand.

She took poor robin redbreast in,
  And bade dear Eva go
And take black pussy off the rug,
  And shut her up below.

And then she laid the shivering bird
  In pussy's place to warm,
For all its feathers dropped with wet,
  From lying in the storm.

And both the little girls sat down
  To watch him as he lay;
And by-and-bye he raised his head—
  And who so pleased as they?

And then he stood upon his feet,
  And slyly looked around,
And pecked a little crumb of cake
  That lay upon the ground.

Then Carry softly left the room,
　　And brought a piece of bread;
And oh! 'twas beautiful to see
　　How robin redbreast fed!

He stood and plumed his pretty breast,
　　And smoothed his shining wing;
Then, flying on a picture-frame,
　　Began to chirp and sing.

But when dear little Eva clapped
　　Her hands and laughed again,
Red robin flew with all his might
　　Against the window-pane.

And Carry said he'd better go,
　　Unless he wished to stay;
And so she raised the sash once more,
　　And off he flew away.

And dear mamma was very pleased
　　When she came home, and heard
How kind her children both had been
　　To that poor frozen bird.

She told them that the God who hears
　　The ravens when they cry,
And stoops from highest heaven to see
　　A little sparrow die,

Looks on the tender-hearted child
　With pleasure and with love;
And when she dies will take her soul
　To dwell with Him above.

SOPHY'S SORROW;

OR, A LESSON FROM LITTLE BIRDS.

WHERE the lovely lilacs wave
　In their leafy glory,
Near an aged oak, that spread
　Wide its branches hoary;

Peering through a tangled growth
　Of ivy-bush and privet,
Stood a joyous-hearted child,
　Little Sophy Knivett.

There a pretty nest she spied,
　With the softest lining,
And the wild convolvulus
　All around it twining.

Three young birds within it chirped,
　And the happy mother
Brought them food, and fed by turns
　One and then another.

B

With a bright, suspicious eye,
　　Oft she watched the stranger,
Lest her little family
　　Haply were in danger.

But when every morn and eve
　　Found Sophia Knivett
Peeping at the pretty nest
　　Through the dark green privet—

Little birdie, bolder grown,
　　Oftentimes came hopping,
Pecking up the crumbs of bread
　　Sophy round was dropping.

And the happy nestlings loved
　　Sophy as a mother,
When she brought them worms, and fed
　　One and then another.

One sweet morn when all things smiled,
　　Why sat Sophy crying?
"Oh!" she sobbed, "my little birds
　　All about are flying!

"They have left the nest, and flown
　　Out of reach for ever;
I shall never feed them more—
　　No, dear mother, never!"

" Dry your tears," her mother said ;
   "Smile away your sadness ;
To think your pretty birds would stay
   In the nest, 'twere madness !

" Better far that they should rise,
   Wide their free flight winging ;
Better far that they should soar
   To the blue sky singing."

Another week, and very ill
   Grew Sophy's baby brother ;
By his cradle all night long
   Watched his weeping mother.

But the pale face whiter grew,
   While she sat there weeping ;
And the little tender babe
   Soon in death was sleeping.

Bitterly though Sophy mourned
   Baby's early dying,
Very much she wished to stay
   Her kind mother's crying.

" Mamma," she said, "'tis very sad
   We and Frank should sever ;
But surely it were wrong to wish
   To keep him here for ever.

" Better far his soul should rise,
　　High its free flight winging;
Better far that he should soar
　　To the blue sky singing!"

So, a lesson from the birds
　　Little Sophy taught her;
And the mother's heart grew calm,
　　Listening to her daughter.

"THE LITTLE MAID."

COME hither now, my little child,
　　And stand beside my knee,
And listen to the pretty tale
　　That I will tell to thee.

In Syria once, the Bible says,
　　There lived, in time of old,
A very rich and mighty man,
　　A soldier strong and bold.

His house was large and beautiful,
　　And filled with splendid things,
For 'twas his pleasant boast to be
　　A favourite of the king's.

But ah! he had a sore disease,
  And could no comfort know;
Poor Naaman in sadness sighed—
  A leper, white as snow.

But once it happened, when he fought,
  And made all hearts afraid,
He brought away from Israel's land
  A little captive maid.

He took her from her friends and home,
  And bore her far away,
To wait upon his stately wife
  Through all the weary day.

Poor little girl! she tried to be
  Contented with her lot,
Though dwelling in a heathen place,
  Where God was worshipped not.

"Alas! poor master!" once she said,
  "I only wish that he
Were living in Samaria's land,
  Where once I used to be!

"For there a mighty prophet dwells,
  And would my lord but go
And see that man of God, he'd cure
  His leprosy, I know."

And somebody told Naaman all
   The captive girl had said;
And seated in his chariot fine,
   To Israel's land he sped.

And soon his horses proud, before
   The prophet's door were seen,
Who bade him seven times to wash
   In Jordan, and be clean.

And Naaman washed; and oh, what joy!
   Away went every sore;
He thanked the prophet's God, and said,
   He'd love Him evermore.

And sure I am, when he went home,
   That everybody smiled,
And praised the God of heaven, and blessed
   The little captive child.

THE HUNGRY BOY.

EAR Marianne and little Jane
    Were dressed to take a ride;
And in their pretty carriage sat,
    So happy, side by side.

For each within her tiny hand
    Held fast a penny bright,
The gift of grandpapa, to spend
    In sugar-plums so white.

The shops were beautiful to see,
    Set out with all the toys
That kind mammas delight to buy
    For careful girls and boys.

Fine horses, with long bushy tails,
    And flowing manes, were there;
Bright yellow parrots, soft as silk,
    And dolls with flaxen hair.

And Marianne and laughing Jane
    Would ask their nurse to stay,
And let them see the pretty things
    That decked the windows gay.

But as they passed a baker's door,
  A ragged boy they met;
He had no shoes upon his feet—
  His cheeks with tears were wet.

And through the window large he looked
  At all the loaves, and said,
"Oh dear! how hungry I do feel—
  I wish I had some bread."

And Marianne grew very sad
  His streaming eyes to see;
"And here's the penny bright," she said,
  "That grandpapa gave me!

"I'll give it to the ragged child,
  Oh, Charlotte, if I may;
I sha'n't be *hungry* if I have
  No sugar-plums to-day."

Nurse gave her leave, and soon the boy
  Dried up his tears, and ran
And bought a nice large penny roll
  Of the big baker's man.

And Marianne told Jane to see
  How fast he ate, and smiled;
And God looked down from heaven and blessed
  The ministering child.

MARY'S DYING DAY.

AIR was the morning—oh ! *so* fair,
    It almost seemed that sin
Was banished from the lovely earth,
    No more to enter in.

O'er hill and stream, and flowery field,
    The happy sunshine smiled,
And little birds in concert sang,
    From tree and hedgerow wild.

Oh, wherefore is the sun so bright,
    And why the flowers so gay,
And little birds so loud in song,
    On Mary's dying day ?

She lies within her darkened room,
    White as the roses pale,
That all around her window hang,
    In clustering beauty frail.

But in her eye there is a light,
    And on her brow a calm,
That speak of holy peace, too deep
    For Death itself to harm.

Then louder sing, ye happy birds,
  And flowers be bright and gay!
Why should ye cease to sing and smile
  On Mary's dying day?

She's passing from a world of change,
  Where sin and sorrow reign,
To dwell in everlasting light,
  Beyond the reach of pain.

For her the white robe is prepared,
  Unsoiled by touch of sin,
And pearly gates are opening wide,
  To let dear Mary in.

Sing, louder sing, ye happy birds,
  And flowers be bright and gay!
For Heaven in sweetest brilliance breaks
  O'er Mary's dying day!

KIND-HEARTED GEORGE.

 POOR old man sat down to eat
A little piece of bread and meat
As Georgy Wright came up the street.

His clothes were torn, his head was bare,
The wind it blew his long white hair,
As cold and friendless he sat there.

"Poor man!" said Georgy, with a sigh,
"I feel that I could almost cry,
You look so thin—I fear you'll die!"

The old man raised his head to hear
Kind words that thrilled his heart and ear,
But down his cheek there rolled a tear.

"Alas!" he said, "if I could see
The gentle boy that speaks to me,
How very happy I should be!

"For dark to me the world has been,
And I have never, never seen
A tree, or flower, or meadow green.

" How often have I wished to view
My mother's face—the skies of blue!
And now I long to look on you."

" Poor man !" said Georgy Wright, " don't cry,
But pray to God that when you die,
Your soul may go to Him on high !

" There you will see, without a tear,
Far better things than we do here,
And, oh ! perhaps your mother dear !"

And little Georgy's words so mild,
Such comfort gave—the old man smiled,
And felt his heavy grief beguiled.

,h:

THE WASHERWOMAN'S CHILD.

HE washerwoman's little girl,
  In summer's scorching heat,
With a great basket in her arms,
  Came toiling up the street.

She put her burden on the ground,
  As tired as could be,
And sat upon a step, and leaned
  Her head upon her knee.

Her weary feet were very sore,
  With walking on the stones,
With all that heavy weight of clothes,
  To take to Mrs. Jones.

And then she closed her aching eyes,
  Half dazzled by the glare;
And, "Oh!" she cried, "I don't know how
  I ever *shall* get there!"

Now Charley Smith was standing near,
  And heard poor Nelly speak;
And he was very grieved to see
  Her look so thin and weak.

"Come, Nelly," said the cheerful boy
  "I'll help you on your way;
I hope it isn't very far
  You have to go to-day."

The grateful girl looked up and said,
  "Oh, thank you!"—with a smile;
And then she sighed, "I really think
  There's yet another mile."

"Oh, well!" cried Charlie, "never mind!"
  And off they went away;
"Oh dear!" exclaimed the willing boy,
  "This *is* a load, I say!"

And soon they stopped to take a rest
  Beneath a shady tree;
And Nelly looked behind, and said,
  "A horse and cart I see!"

And when the driver nearer came,
  "Oh, please, sir," Charley cried,
"Let Mrs. Lather's tired girl
  Have just a little ride!"

The man was kind, and stopped the horse,
  And, "Come along," said he;
"Give me your hand, my little maid,
  And sit in front with me."

Then Charley held the basket up,
   Which soon was placed behind,
And man and horse, and girl and clothes,
   Went forward like the wind!

And then that ever cheerful child
   Went home to have his tea,
And, oh! he felt within his heart
   As happy as could be.

"For better 'twas," his mother said,
   When he his story told,
"To help the weary, than to have
   A pocketful of gold."

LOST BOBBY;

OR, THE BROADSTAIRS TRAGEDY.

OOR Mrs. Green was very ill,
    And grew so thin and weak,
There was no brightness in her eye,
    No colour in her cheek;
And Dr. Camomile, he said,
    As physic did no good,
Perhaps a little change of air,
    A trip to Broadstairs, would.

And so at once she started off
    With Caroline and Ann,
Old Martha and the baby twins,
    And Georgy, Bob, and Fan;
And when they felt the cooling breeze
    Upon the ocean wide,
" How pleasant 'tis," said Mrs. Green,
    "To being in Cheapside!"

Next morning, on the sunny sands,
    The children romped in glee,
And both the little babies crowed
    Upon old Martha's knee;

But Mrs. Green was much fatigued,
　And had an aching head,
And so she thought she'd better rest,
　And breakfast in her bed.

Grave Caroline her basket took,
　And strolled along the shore,
To gather shells and seaweed strange
　She'd never seen before;
And Ann, with shoes and stockings off,
　Ran gaily in the tide,
While George, and Bob, and Fanny played
　With sand, by nurse's side.

But all at once there came a shriek
　From Annie in her play;
"Oh, Martha! come, a dreadful wave
　Has washed my shoes away!"
So poor old nurse, as quick as thought,
　Threw off her snow-white shawl,
And on it laid the twins, beneath
　Her big brown parasol.

And then she snatched up George's spade,
　And hurried down to Ann,
Who, all impatient, shouted out,
　"Run faster, if you can!"

And bravely through the great green waves
  Did breathless Martha wade,
Until the floating shoes she reached
  With Master George's spade.

Then, dripping wet, she hastened back
  To where the infants lay,
Who both kicked off their scarlet shoes
  While nursey was away;
And missing that devoted friend,
  A piteous wail began,
And stuffed their fists into their mouths,
  As only babies can!

She hushed them to her faithful breast,
  And, rocking to and fro,
Sang "By, O baby," to the tune
  That only nurses know.
But suddenly the song was changed
  To screams of "Georgie, here!—
All of a trimble I do feel—
  I don't see Bobby near!"

Said George, "When you went after Ann,
  He said he would not stay;
He threw some sand in Fanny's eyes,
  And then he ran away."

Old Martha rose in wild affright,
   " Oh, *where* can Bobby be ?
Perhaps he's fallen off the cliff,
   Or drownded in the sea."

With bitter tears and loud regrets,
   She gave the babes to Ann,
Then, up and down the sandy beach
   The poor old woman ran.
She searched the caves, she scratched the heaps
   Of seaweed as they lay—
" Afeared each moment," as she said,
   "To see poor Bobby's clay."

She moved and lifted heavy stones,
   Till scarcely she could breathe,
" Because, maybe, his tender bones
   Are lyin' underneathe."
She called his name with piteous cries,
   And made a dreadful stir ;
Two nursemaids almost lost their babes
   By running after her !

To think she'd lived to see the day
   She'd break it to his ma,
The flower of the flock was gone,
   The image of his pa !

That very selfsame pa, who said,
    He'd soon be comin' down,
If Bobby was but good, and bring
    Some lollipops from town.

Worn out and sad, the hungry twins
    At last she homeward bore,
Who thrust their fists into their mouths
    More fiercely than before.
Close clinging to her dabbled skirts,
    The younger children ran;
While sobbing mournfully behind
    Came Caroline and Ann.

When Mrs. Green the tidings heard,
    'Twas thought she would have died;
She had no strength to speak, but just
    To whisper, "Have him cried."
And then she fainted right away,
    Quite overwhelmed with grief,
Till Dr. Water's lotion gave
    Her aching head relief.

Now soon the crier's bell was heard
    Upon the long parade:
"Lost, on the sands, at 12 this day—
    Or, maybe, stole or strayed—

" Well, just at five o'clock was heard
The sound of tramping feet,
Of men and women, boys and girls,
All hastening down the street."

A little boy, in lightish boots,
  And jacket of nankeen,
Dark hair, and answers to the name
  Of Master Robert Green.

" His eyes are black, his cheeks are red,
  His frock is somewhat tore ;
He's lately lost a finger-nail,
  Through jamming in a door.
And whosoever brings him back
  To Barfield Lodge, shall be
Rewarded with a thousand thanks,
  Beside a handsome fee."

That afternoon the town was searched,
  And everywhere they sent,
" Wherever," as old Martha said,
  " Poor Bobby *might* have went."
One hope alone her bosom cheered—
  " He'll find his home," said she,
" If livin', 'cos he knowed his ma
  Had promised shrimps for tea ! "

Well, just at five o'clock was heard
  The sound of tramping feet,
Of men and women, boys and girls,
  All hastening down the street.

Old nursey, bonnetless, rushed out,
    And screamed with rapture loud,—
" 'Tis Bobby, on a donkey's back,
    A comin' in the crowd !"

Then in again, upstairs she sped—
    " Oh, missus, Bobby's found !
A little paler than before,
    But elsewhere safe and sound."
Poor Mrs. Green looked up and smiled,
    And faintly said, " I heard ;
Don't wake the babes !" then closed her eyes,
    Nor spoke another word.

Oh ! 'twas, indeed, a sight to move
    A mother's heart, to see
Young Bobby clutched in nurse's arms,
    And struggling to be free ;
And all the children clinging round,
    And tugging at her gown,—
" We want to ask him where he's been ;
    Oh, Martha, put him down."

Then spoke the ragged donkey boy,—
    " I found him all forlorn,
A cryin' in a field of wheat,
    Half choked of eatin' corn ;

'Now tell me where you lives,' says I,
  'And you shall have a ride;'
And then he dried his eyes, and said,
  'In London, at Chipside.'

"I took him up to mother's house,
  Not fur from Ramsgate Pier,
And giv' him bread and cheese to eat,
  And half a mug o' beer;
But couldn't find his lodgin's out,
  Altho' we struggled hard,
Till turning of his pockets out,
  We come to Cantfell's card.

"And mother in a twinklin' knowed
  That was a Broadstair name;—
I never stopped to hear no more,
  But right away I came.
I got old Neddy to the door,
  And popped him on his back,
Jumped up behind, and home agin
  I brought him in a crack."

And nursey said 'twas very like
  He'd "get a silver crown;
But call to-morrow night, 'cos then
  Bob's pa was coming down."

And then she shook his sunburnt hand,
    And said, with tears of joy,
" If there was Christians on the earth,
    'Twas that there donkey boy."

THE LITTLE OLD WOMAN.

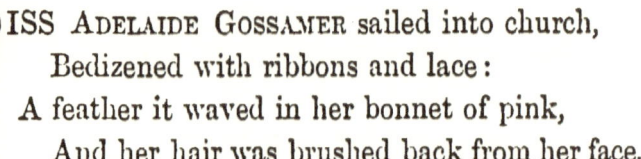

ISS Adelaide Gossamer sailed into church,
    Bedizened with ribbons and lace :
A feather it waved in her bonnet of pink,
    And her hair was brushed back from her face.

And rudely by neat little Mary she swept,
    And proudly flounced into her pew,
With a toss of the head, and a look that ex-
      pressed,
    " I'm very much finer than you ! "

It happened that morning a minister preached
    Whom many delighted to hear,
And hundreds of people, his sermons who loved,
    Were thronging from far and from near.

Among them a little old woman came in,
    And slowly walked up the long aisle,
Then taking her stand by gay Adelaide's pew,
    She leaned on the door for a while.

And Adelaide pouted, and looked very grand,
   And spread out her dress with a sneer,
That seemed to the tired old woman to say,
   "Don't think that you're coming in here."

But neat little Mary her Bible had read,
   Which told her that pride was a sin;
So kindly and softly she opened her pew,
   And beckoned the old woman in.

Now just as the minister finished, and sent
   His large congregation away,
And Adelaide turned with contempt to observe
   Kind Mary's neat mantle of grey—

A loud clap of thunder was heard in the air,
   And the grateful old woman she said,—
"I think, little Miss, there's a storm coming on,
   For dark are the clouds overhead.

"You pitied a feeble old woman, and now
   A speedy reward you will gain;
My biggest umbrella I've luckily brought,
   And both it will shield from the rain."

And true were her words, for they had not gone far,
   When down fell the raindrops apace;
But Mary was sheltered, and soon arrived home,
   Quite dry, with a smile on her face.

But *Adelaide!* oh, had you seen her pass by,
  The sight you could never forget:
The colour it streamed from her bonnet of pink,
  And her feather was dripping with wet.

Her pale yellow gloves and her light parasol
  Were speedily spoilt by the rain;
And her gay trailing dress was so dabbled with mire,
  She never could wear it again!

"And oh," exclaimed Mary, "how thankful I feel"
  (As Adelaide passed from her view)
"That I pitied the poor little woman, so pale,
  And gave her a seat in our pew."

THE SCHOOL TREAT.

OUR tables long with clean white cloths,
  And buns and cakes, were spread;
The room was dressed with flowers, and flags
  Were waving overhead.

And boys and girls came thronging round,
  All washed and combed and neat—
They were the children of the school,
  And this their yearly treat.

And very pleasant 'twas to see
  Each happy, shining face,
And hear their voices when they stood
  And sang their pretty grace.

And then the busy teachers went
  Among them, here and there,
With tea, and cakes, and buns, till all
  Had plenty and to spare.

And while we watched that active band,
  How glad we felt to see
Two happy little children, kind,
  Handing the mugs of tea.

Their smiling faces seemed to say,
　　As loud as words, I'm sure,
"Oh, what a pleasant thing it is
　　To feed the hungry poor!"

"Ah!" thought I, "when the busy scenes
　　Of life shall be no more,
And those two little girls shall stand
　　Upon the unknown shore—

"May Fanny and may Alice find
　　These words their joy to be,—
'Ye did it to the least of these,
　　And therefore unto Me.'"

THE DEAD BABY.

T was a very solemn day
　　When little baby died,
And dear papa and dear mamma
　　Were very sad, and cried.

She was so young—this wicked
　　world
Her feet had never trod;
And yet her gentle soul was called
　　To go and live with God.

Pale was she as the rosebud white
  Within her tiny hand;
Cold as the snow, that never falls
  Upon the better land.

And she was in that lovely land,
  The white-winged angels' home,
Where all the little lambs of Christ
  One day shall surely come.

And very well her parents knew
  That she was safely there,
But yet they felt 'twas hard to part
  With that sweet infant fair.

And as they sat, and sadly wept,
  Within the darkened room,
A little child came like a beam
  Of sunshine in the gloom.

She quickly climbed their knees, and said,
  "Oh no! you must not cry:
For little baby's gone to live
  With Jesus, in the sky."

And smiles upon their faces came,
  Though still in grief they bowed,
Just as you've noticed, in a storm,
  A rainbow in the cloud.

THE BUNCH OF GRAPES.

BEAUTIFUL grapes, mamma; *oh*, what a treat!
Don't they look tempting! and won't they be
    sweet!
Good Mr. Harvey, how kind he must be,
To send such a present to Lucy and me!

"Now, Lucy, don't *snatch* them; but wait for
    your share—
She's swallowed some down—skins and all, I
    declare;
That's right, dear mamma, move them out of her
    way,
Or she'll eat up her own and mine too, I dare
    say!"

Mamma took her scissors, the grapes to divide,
Then looked at the fine purple cluster, and sighed;
"There's poor Mary Morgan so sadly," said she,
"How grateful for some of these grapes she would be!

"She lies on her pillow, so thirsty and weak,
With a bright crimson spot on her poor wasted cheek;
And her lips are so parched, that I'm sure 'twould be kind
To send her a few, if you felt so inclined."

But Lucy was greedy, and shouted " No, no ! "
But Minnie too sorry she felt to do so.
She looked at the grapes—then she nodded her head,
And "Take mine to poor thirsty Mary," she said.

That night, just as Minnie had finished her prayers,
Papa and mamma were seen coming upstairs,
With a beautiful kitten, as white as the snow,
With a blue ribbon tied round its neck with a bow.

"And this," said papa, " is a present I've brought
To the dear little girl who did as she ought,
Who gave up her grapes with a hearty good-will
To poor little Mary, so thirsty and ill."

SULKY TOM.

E was a cross old cat,
  With great round eyes of green,
And stripes of black all down his back,
  And yellow marks between.

He ne'er was heard to purr,
  ·And never seen to play;
And if you stroked him on the head,
  He growled and walked away.

But, oh! how sulky Tom
  (For that was pussy's name)
Did wag his long and angry tail
  When the new servant came!

He sat before the fire,
  And rolled his wicked eye,
And clawed and spit, if just her gown
  Should touch him passing by.

And so Eliza said,
  "I'll make you feel for that!
There, take that box upon your ears,
  You bad, ill-tempered cat!"

And then she turned him out,
  And slammed the kitchen door,
And said "she'd teach him pretty quick
  To serve her so no more!"

Well, sulky Tom he sat
  Upon the stones outside;
And very hungry he became,
  And very cold beside.

His friend, the cook, was gone;
  So, very sad was he,
For he was driven from the fire,
  Without his milk for tea.

He couldn't sit and starve,
  And so he grew a thief;
The safe door stood ajar, and Tom
  Got in and gnawed the beef.

And next he dragged it all
  Right down upon the stones,
And ate so fast, that at the last
  Was nothing left but bones!

Now just as Tom had done,
  Loud rang the parlour bell,
And "Lay the supper," mistress said,
  "And bring the beef as well."

But when Eliza went
    Outside to fetch the meat,
Oh dear! the bones and sulky Tom
    Were lying at her feet!

She ran and fetched the broom,
    And beat him on the head;
And poor old sulky Tom he mewed,
    As if he'd soon be dead.

But by-and-bye he rose,
    And slowly walked away,
And crawled from there to Lonsdale Square,
    And in the garden lay.

He lay there all the night,
    And till the morning came,
When girls and boys ran trooping in
    To have a pleasant game.

And soon upon the ground
    Poor pussy they espied,
Whose head was still so very sore,
    That when 'twas stroked he cried.

From Mary Winter's eyes
    The tears began to flow,
And, " Oh!" she said, "some wicked boys
    Have beaten you, I know!

Sulky Tom.

"There, pussy, don't you cry,
    And I will take you home,
And give you meat and bread to eat,
    Where wicked boys don't come."

And sulky Tom he seemed
    To know that she was kind,
And didn't growl at all—nor wag
    His yellow tail behind!

She took him in her arms
    To dear mamma, who said,
"That though he was an ugly cat,
    He might be housed and fed."

And cook, she too was kind,
    And to the pantry went,
And in a saucer poured some milk,
    To Mary's great content.

And sulky Tom he drank
    As though he'd never tire;
And for the first time in his life,
    He purred before the fire.

ROBIN REDBREAST.

HE bleak winds are blowing, the snow's falling
    fast ;
The cattle in vain seek their meadow repast.

The starved ruffled sparrows are drooping their
    wings,
But Robin—he sits on a dry bough, and sings !

Oh ! beautiful songster ! alone on the tree,
How lovely a lesson thou teachest to me !

If thou canst sing on when the summer is
    past,
And thickly around thee the snow falleth fast,

Should *I* not be cheerful, with food and with fire ;
With clothing, and shelter, and all I desire ?

And must I not offer, sweet Robin, like thee,
My thanks to the Giver of good things to me ?

Oh ! come to my window ! do come and be fed ;
And every morning I'll sprinkle some bread,

To feed thee, dear Robin, till winter is past,
And beautiful spring-time comes smiling at last.

FREDDY HODGE;

OR, THE LITTLE LAMB.

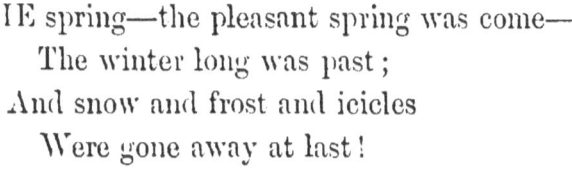

HE spring—the pleasant spring was come—
    The winter long was past;
And snow and frost and icicles
    Were gone away at last!

And pretty violets, sweet and blue,
    Among the grass were seen;
And primroses came peeping out
    From folded leaves of green.

The skylark mounting in the air
    Poured forth her cheerful strain,
As Freddy Hodge, just out of school,
    Came down the pleasant lane.

Now Freddy was as nice a boy
    As any one could find,
Who from his babyhood had been
    To poor dumb creatures kind.

He never trod upon a snail,
    Nor pinched a little fly;
Nor pulled poor harmless pussy's tail
    When nobody was by.

And, as he gaily trudged along,
    How very pleased was he
To hear the great rooks cawing loud
    On every lofty tree !

But soon, no more his heart rejoiced
    To hear their ceaseless caw ;
For, lying helpless in a ditch,
    A little lamb he saw.

It struggled hard to climb the bank,
    But down again it went ;
And then all quietly it lay,
    As if its strength were spent.

Its mother through the hedgerow looked,
    And bleated very sore ;
Till Freddy's feeling heart could bear
    Her piteous cries no more.

And oh ! he thought, one day I hope
    To be a big, brave man !
And shall I not, while I am young,
    Do always what I can ?

There's not much water in the ditch,
    Because there's been no rain ;
And sure I am, I'm strong enough
    To scramble out again.

So Freddy carefully went down,
  And reached the helpless lamb,
Then clambered up the mossy bank,
  And laid it by its dam.

The grateful creature licked his hand,
  And then she cried no more ;
And Freddy trembled with delight,
  He'd never known before.

And down again he quickly came,
  Then up the other side ;
And soon at home, before the fire,
  His socks and shoes he dried.

And poor old Ann, the nurse, she stood
  And softly stroked his head ;
Exclaiming, as she heard his tale,
  " God bless you, Master Fred ! "

And Freddy took her down the lane
  To see the place next day,
And there inside the field they saw
  The little lamb at play.

CHRISTMAS DAY;

OR, POOR PEGGY'S TUMBLE.

'TWAS Christmas Eve! the roads were hard,
  The sky was clear and cold,
And from its cloudless arch looked down
  Ten thousand stars of gold.

And on the sparkling, frosty earth
  The lovely moonbeams lay,
You might have fancied diamond dust
  Was strewed along the way.

And sweetly on the evening air
  Arose the voice of song;
Band after band of choristers
  Came singing all night long.

Tucked warmly in their little beds,
  Young Jane and Martha lay,
And heard them sing how Jesus Christ
  Was born on Christmas Day.

And when afar sweet voices told
  Of God's good-will to men,
"It is the angels," Martha said,
  "Come down to earth again."

They listened till the music fled,
　　Then soundly slept, nor woke
Till in the rosy eastern sky
　　The cold, bright morning broke.

Oh! cheery is the Christmas morn,
　　And sweet it is to hear
The merry church-bells' birthday chime
　　For Christ our Saviour dear.

To Martha and to Jane they seemed
　　To say, "Oh, come and sing
About the babe of Bethlehem,
　　About the 'new-born King.'"

And soon the happy little girls
　　To church were on their way,
Each with a Bible in her hand,
　　Bought new for Christmas Day.

And though the sleet began to fall,
　　They did not mind it; *no*,
For they were wrapt in scarlet cloaks,
　　And not "afraid of snow."

The church with holly-boughs was drest,
　　And here and there were seen
The Laurustinus' clustered flowers,
　　In wreaths of ivy green.

And dear papa and dear mamma
 Were there to sing and pray;
For all good people love to go
 To church on Christmas Day.

The service done, all homeward went
 As quickly as they might,
For naughty boys were making slides
 Along the pavement white.

Close holding by their parents' hands,
 The children reached their door,
When poor old Peggy slipped and fell,
 Who slowly walked before.

Now Peggy had not been to church,
 Because she loved it not,
For she was fond of evil ways,
 And oft her God forgot.

But dear papa and dear mamma,
 They ever bore in mind
That Jesus Christ to wicked folks
 As well as good was kind.

And so they took poor Peggy in,
 Brushed off the snow and dirt;
And then for Dr. Hardy sent,
 To see if she was hurt.

Poor Peggy said she'd "broke her leg;"
  The Doctor he said "No;
She'd had a shaking in the fall,
  And got a bruise or so."

Still, in the hall she wrung her hands,
  And wept big tears of grief;
"Oh, what's the matter?" Martha said;
  Says she, "I smells the beef!"

Says little Mike, who joined the group,
  "It's more than *that* you smell;
There's a big turkey by the fire,
  And sausages as well!"

Then in the parlour, to mamma,
  Did little Martha run;
And, "Let me give my beef," she cried,
  "To Peggy, who has none!"

"And half my pudding," Jane exclaimed,
  "I'll give her, if I may;
Because the slice is always large
  I have on Christmas Day."

And good papa he smiled, and said,
  "He'd cut her off some meat;
And she should have some pudding, too,
  A real Christmas treat."

And Peggy dined, and wiped the tears
    From off her cheeks so brown,
And said that she should "bless the day
    She'd ever tumbled down."

With many thanks she left the house—
    But, ah! how sad to say,
Mamma's goloshes, in the hall,
    Were seen not from *that* day!

THE CHURCH MOUSE.

ON Sundays, little reader, when I was young as
    you,
My seat was in the corner of a high old-
    fashioned pew.

This pew it had a lining of somewhat faded
    green,
And all along its edges brass-headed nails were
    seen.

The lining in my corner was ragged here and
    there,
And looked in many places a great deal "worse
    for wear."

One morning, as I listened to what the preacher said,
A little hungry mousey, brown, skinny, and ill-fed,

Came creeping through the lining, beneath my cloak, and
    clung
Close to my silken waistband—till I got home it hung.

I took it to my bedroom as quickly as I could,
And put it on a candle that on my table stood.

And mousey he went nibbling as fast as he could eat,
As if he thought the tallow a most delicious treat.

Then in a box I placed him, with nice soft wool and hay,
And mousey he got fatter and tamer every day.

Sometimes the lid I'd open, and in and out he'd run,
And take a merry scamper across the floor in fun!

Month after month I kept him, as happy as could be,
And very much I loved him, for he was fond of me.

But, ah! one dreadful morning, upstairs there creeping came
A little naughty fellow (I shall not tell his name);

And mousey's box he opened, and drove him all about,
While I was in the parlour, and knew not he was out.

The little frightened creature ran wildly o'er the floor,
Then darted quick as lightning outside the open door.

And then that boy so wicked, he left his cruel fun,—
But not a word he told us of all that he had done.

Now Snow, the great white pussy, upon the stairs he sat,
And thought he heard a mousey, or else he "smelt a rat."

And up he went so softly, to take a glance around,
And, hiding in a corner, the little mouse he found.

He seized him in a moment, and bit him in the side,
And hurt him so severely, that soon poor mousey died!

And then that boy so cruel, it very soon was known
That he had dared to meddle with what was not his own.

He said he hadn't touched it, but, ah! his cheek grew red;
And so he had no supper, was whipped, and sent to bed.

MINNIE'S FAVOURITES.

YOU'RE standing in the sunshine, Minnie,
    Standing laughing there;
Frolicsome as is the breeze
    That lifts your golden hair;

You're standing in the sunshine, Minnie,
    Flinging on the ground
Corn to feed your feathered pets,
    Flocking gladly round.

The cock, with golden plumage, Minnie,
    And tail of glossy green,
Stands at your feet—as bold a fowl
    As ever could be seen.

He eats the grain you scatter, Minnie,
    Then begins to crow,
As if he said, " I'm much obliged
    For all the food you throw."

Pleasant is it, little Minnie,
    Pleasant to be kind!
He who can neglect the dumb
    Must have a cruel mind.

E

Let your life be love, my Minnie,
   So one day you'll stand—
In fuller, holier sunshine sweet—
   Within the better land.

PRAYING TOM.

SPRIGHTLY little African
   Was taken for a slave,
And carried in a crowded ship
   Across the briny wave.

They stole him as he soundly slept
   Beneath the date tree wild,
And vainly both his parents sought
   Their dear and absent child.

Poor little Tom ! they landed him
   Upon a stranger shore,
And never, never might he see
   His native country more !

But ah ! how very sweet to tell,
   To that far shore, one day,
A pious missionary came,
   To read, and preach, and pray.

And to the weeping slaves he spoke
  About a home of love;
A place where partings are unknown,
  A world of joy above!

And little Tom he listening sat,
  Nor lost a single word,
Till all about the life and death
  Of Jesus Christ he heard.

Next morning, as the teacher passed,
  He heard poor Tommy pray,
" Lord Jesus, send some men to steal
  My parents dear away.

" And bring them hither in a ship
  Across the mighty sea,
That I may tell them all the things
  The good man told of Thee."

Then down the shingly beach he ran,
  And gazed across the tide,
In hope some stately ship to see
  Come o'er the waters wide.

The teacher, who had followed, asked,
  " Why are you watching there ? "
" I look," said little Tom, " to see
  If Jesus answers prayer."

Week after week, month after month,
  He gazed across the foam ;
Two years had passed—his parents still
  Dwelt in their sunny home.

But as he watched, with hopeful heart,
  One morning, on the strand,
There came a vessel filled with slaves
  From Tommy's native land !

Oh ! who can ever paint the joy
  Of Afric's tawny child !
His heart beat high—and from his lips
  Came bursts of rapture wild !

Sometimes he leaped upon the shore,
  Then dashed into the spray,
As if he wished to help the boats
  More swiftly on their way !

Stroke after stroke—stroke after stroke !
  And now they near the land !
A few long moments more—and then
  Dark faces throng the strand !

And Tommy, speechless, clasps the knees
  Of both his parents there,
While thanks are gushing from his heart
  To Him who answers prayer.

CHILDREN IN HEAVEN.

HAD a dream—I heard them sing—
  The little children dear,
Grouped on the everlasting hills
  In yonder sunny sphere.

The bloom was on their cherub cheeks,
  And clouds of golden hair
Were shading every beauteous brow,
  As they stood singing there.

I saw the white-robed angels' hands
  Pause on the glowing string;
I heard them hush their mighty strains,
  To let the children sing.

Oh, wild, sweet anthem! while it rose,
  Nor breeze nor leaflet stirred;
Only the ripple of Life's wave
  In symphony was heard.

There was a little child I knew
  Among that blessed throng;
My very heart was thrilled with joy
  To hear *her* voice in song!

I knew her by her polished brow,
    So strangely calm and fair;
I knew her by her eyes of blue,
    And gold-besprinkled hair.

I knew her by the rosebud white
    Her hands in death had pressed;
Now bursting into fragrant flower
    Upon her gentle breast.

And all her song was love to Him
    Who once, a sinless child,
Left the sweet summer of the skies,
    For earth's cold winter wild;

Who walked the world with weary feet,
    And pain and hunger bore;
And died a shameful death, that she
    Might live for evermore!

O child of mine! to glory gone!
    Through whirling tempest drear—
Like song of bird in noisy street,
    Thy thrilling voice I hear!

Though hushed the music—fled the dream—
    Its echoes linger still;
And harp-notes float at intervals
    From Zion's holy hill.

Oh! when the deafening storms of earth
    Are stilled, may I and mine,
In the sweet calm of heaven unite
    Our songs of praise with thine!

THE GOD WHO MADE THE SHELLS.

H, tiny shells! how sweet the truth
    Your shining beauty tells!
The Lord of all, who rules the skies,
Clothed you with pearl and rainbow dyes;
Must He not tender be, as wise,
    The God who made the shells?

Oh, say not how His red right arm
    In dreadful strength excels!
For here His loveliness I see,
And think, Can *I* uncared-for be,
When the same hand which fashioned me
    Was that which made the shells?

Each fragile arch He stooped to mould,
    Who high in glory dwells;
He gemmed old Ocean's glittering floor,
Strewed your sweet tints o'er rock and shore;
And in your radiance I'll adore
    The God who made the shells!

A SICK MOTHER TO HER CHILDREN.

M Y children dear, day after day,
　　In pain and sadness deep,
In weakness on my couch I lie,
While weary hours pass slowly by,
　　And nights that know not sleep.

Through the closed blinds the summer sun
　　Is streaming pure and bright:
Ah! *once* I loved its lustre well,
But now my aching eyelids tell
　　I cannot bear its light!

I hear the careless merriment
　　Of children at their play,
And once, like them, *I* was a child,
Of bounding step and laughter wild,
　　But all has passed away!

Oh! precious gifts ye surely were
　　To me from Love Divine,
But since I clasped you to my breast,
And glowing faces fondly pressed,
　　The roses died on mine.

And when upon your golden heads
   My wasted hands I lay,
I sometimes tremble lest ye find
The world inconstant and unkind,
   If I am called away.

For in my heart dwells love for you
   Too deep for words to tell;
So that I think my tears would flow,
Even in heaven, if I should know
   It did not use you well.

Kneel down, my little ones, kneel down !
   And let us ask in prayer,
That He who rules the hosts above
Would guard with more than mother's love
   The babes that seek His care.

Ah ! were it not that Jesus lives,
   It would be drear to die !
But He who loved to bless and fold
Dear children in His arms of old,
   Can parents' place supply.

And if He call me hence, perhaps
   Sometimes He'll let me come
To kiss you in your quiet sleep,
And whisper of the mysteries deep
   Of my eternal home !

And ye shall in your slumbers smile,
　The while you sweetly dream
Of harps of gold, and clustering bowers,
And glorious trees, and fadeless flowers,
　Beside Life's sunny stream.

But if, shut in with God in heaven,
　This may not—cannot be,
Beneath His wings may you repose,
Whose wakeful eye no slumber knows,
　To all eternity!

Yes! cling to Him, my darlings, cling,
　From childhood's earliest days;
So on the everlasting shore
We'll meet, where partings are no more,
　And sing His boundless praise.

THE ORPHAN COMFORTED.

SAD and still sits little Mary,
    On the mossy churchyard wall,
With the dying leaves around her
    Dropping from the elm tree tall.

Why so sad sits little Mary,
    With her gentle cheek so pale?
Ah! the crape-folds on her bonnet
    Tell, alas! a mournful tale!

On the new-made grave beneath her
    Oft she drops the scalding tear!
There in solemn sleep are lying
    Father kind, and mother dear!

Oh! that mother's loving glances!
    Never will she meet them more!
Never bound to greet her father,
    Hastening home—day's labour o'er.

Effie's coming up the meadow!
    Rosy Effie, robed in white,
Flinging crimson sorrel blossoms
    At her nurse with wild delight.

When she reaches little Mary,
    Why does Effie laugh no more ?
Ah ! she sees the lonely orphan
    Has been weeping very sore.

Not a word she speaks in passing,
    But she often looks behind,
Watching Mary's poor black tippet
    Flapping in the autumn wind.

Effie reaches home in silence,
    Thinking of that child forlorn ;
And mamma inquires, with wonder,
    Where her merry smiles are gone.

Then with bursting tears she answers,
    " Mary Robins sits to cry
By the new grave in the churchyard,
    Where her poor dead parents lie.

" Oh, mamma ! let little Mary
    Sometimes come and play with me,—
Help me weed my pretty garden,
    Swing me 'neath the chestnut tree.

" Let us read sweet tales together,
    Ride about on Dapple-grey,
Gather wild flowers in the orchard,
    Listening to the blackbird's lay."

" Sad and still sits little Mary,
    On the mossy churchyard wall,
With the dying leaves around her
    Dropping from the elm tree tall."

Good mamma with kindness promised
   She should on the morrow come;
And at early morning Effie
   Fetched her to her happy home.

Oh! what sunshine after showers!
   How they talked, and read, and played!
And mamma trained gentle Mary
   To be Effie's little maid.

To the new grave in the churchyard
   Effie would with Mary go,
Bearing clustering roots of snowdrops
   That would in the spring-time blow.

And when Spring's sweet face came smiling,
   Truly on that mound were seen
Full a hundred pure white blossoms,
   Trembling 'mid their leaves of green.

And the little girls would watch them,
   Sitting on the mossy wall,
With the tender leaves above them
   Shooting from the elm tree tall.

They would sit and talk together
   Of that day, with deep delight,
When the dead should rise in beauty,
   Like the snowdrops, clothed in white.

And the grateful thanks of Mary
　To the orphan's Friend would rise,
Who had dried her tears when weeping
　Dear ones passed into the skies.

THE EAGLE'S ROCK.

T was the Golden Eagle's Rock,
　Craggy, and wild, and lone,
Where he sat in state, with his royal mate,
　On his undisputed throne.

High on the dizzy steep
　Did their blood-stained eyrie lie,
Where the white bones told who had robbed
　　　the fold,
　When the shepherd was not by.

Well might the spoilers gloat
　At ease in their fortress grey,
For never had man, since the world began,
　Clambered its height halfway.

And the Golden Eagle stood
　Eyeing the noonday sun,
Till the clamouring cry of his nestlings nigh
　Charged him with work undone.

And his mighty wings are spread,
  And he sweepeth down chasms wide;
And his fierce eyes gleam by the mountain stream,
  And he scours the hill's green side.

Then o'er a shady glen
  Doth the bold marauder sail,
Where villagers gay hold a festal day,
  Down in their verdant vale.

Apart from a joyous group,
  A mother her darling bears;
With happy smiles at his baby wiles,
  His innocent mirth she shares.

Then she sits on the velvet sward,
  Shaded by trees at noon,
And rocks him to rest on her loving breast,
  Singing a low, sweet tune.

Now on the soft green turf
  That mother her babe doth lie,
While over its head is a watcher dread,
  In that dark spot in the sky.

She kisses its cherub cheek,
  And leaves it awhile—ah, woe!
For broader above, o'er her gentle dove,
  That terrible spot doth grow.

F

Hushed was the peasants' mirth,
  And the stoutest they stood aghast,
And the wail of despair it rent the air,
  As the eagle o'er them passed.

He has stolen the pretty child,
  All in its rosy sleep;
And bears it in might, with ponderous flight,
  Straight towards his castle keep!

Whose is that upturned face,
  White as the mountain snow?
Horror is there, and blank despair,
  Speechless and tearless woe.

Pale are those bloodless lips;
  But lo! in that mother's eye
There flasheth the light of love's great might,
  Stronger than agony.

She darts from the wailing throng,
  Her coming is like the wind!
The weeping loud of the noisy crowd
  Dieth away behind.

She rusheth o'er field and fell,
  Her footsteps at hindrance mock;
She startles the snake in the rustling brake,
  And reacheth the Eagle's Rock.

Mother, go home and weep;
   What canst thou farther do?
Over thy head, immense and dread,
   Frowneth the mountain blue.

Sorrow hath made her mad,
   She scaleth the rough rock's side,—
Now on the edge of a shelving ledge,
   And now on a platform wide.

Onward and upward still,
   Scarce does she pause for breath;
Woman, beware! thou hast not there
   "A step between thee and death!"

Scrambling up fearful crags,
   Still doth she higher go;
Close let her cling! for the loose stones ring
   Clattering to depths below.

First of the breathless crowds,
   Flocking in haste beneath,
A son of the wave, high-souled and brave,
   Dashes across the heath.

He follows her upward flight,
   Yes, till his eyes grow dim:
In the fierce storm-blast he has topped the mast,
   But this is no place for him.

So he must softly creep
　　Down from the heights above;
His heart it is true, but he never knew
　　The might of a mother's love.

Higher she mounts! she climbs
　　Where the wild goat fears to stand;
Death follows behind—fleet, fleet as the wind,
　　Still she eludes his hand.

She reached the fearful wall,
　　Under the great rock's brow,
Where the ivy has clung and has swayed and swung
　　From earliest time till now.

Clambering the network old,
　　Which its twining stems have wrought,
She wrestles in prayer with her Maker there—
　　Doth "she fear God for nought"?

Niagara's awful flood
　　Is spanned by a glorious bow;
And Joy she springs, on her sunny wings,
　　From the blackest tide of woe!

And the cry of that mother's heart
　　Is heard, and her faith is blest;
For with rapture wild, she hath snatched her child,
　　Unharmed, from the eagle's nest.

Flapping their dusky wings,
  Fiercely the spoilers came;
She heard their screams, and she saw the gleams
  That shot from their eyes of flame!

Like spirits of evil, foul,
  They circled around her head;
Then, yelling aloud, amazed and cowed,
  Down the steep rock they fled.

Close to her throbbing heart
  She bindeth her weeping child;
She wipeth its tears, and she quells its fears,
  Up in that region wild.

And she blesses the Mighty Hand
  That carried her there, and knows
That aid shall be lent, through the dread descent,
  To that terrible journey's close.

Hush! down the rifted rock
  She beareth her burden sweet;
No might of her own maketh fast each stone
  Firmly beneath her feet.

She trusts, and her bleeding hands
  Safely the ivy grasp,
For a spirit of love, from her God above,
  Is strengthening it in her clasp.

Lower she comes, and sees
   Beneath her a mountain lamb,
That, cautious and slow, to the vale below
   Follows its careful dam.

And she tracketh, with thankful heart,
   The path of her gentle guide,
Whose feet will be found on the surest ground,
   Down the steep mountain's side.

Hark! from the plain beneath,
   Voices are rising loud!
The shout and the cheer, they have reached her ear,
   And she sees the breathless crowd.

Louder, and louder still,
   Swelleth the welcome strain:
"Oh, loving heart! thou hast done thy part—
   Return to thy rest again!"

She reacheth the mountain's foot—
   Hurrah! for her task is o'er:
And the deed she hath done hath a tribute won
   Of praises for evermore.

And a lesson she taught to all,
   Of energy, faith, and love;—
Hast thou the right? stand up and fight—
   Looking to God above.

Shame on ye, timid souls!
　Feeble for aught but ill;
Shall sin and shall woe waste this world below,
　And will ye lie sluggish still?

Wrest from their grasp the prey,
　Crush them, though cowards mock!
And if the heart quail and the courage fail,
　Think of the Eagle's Rock!

THE AGED BEGGAR;

OR, THE SNOW STORM.

HIGH blazed the wood-piled nursery fire,
　And rosy children four
Were playing in its cheerful glow,
　Upon the toy-strewn floor.

But Bessie sat apart from all,
　In meditation still,
Watching the snow-flakes gently melt
　Upon the window-sill.

First, "few and far between" they fell:
　To Bessie's eager eyes,
Stray feathers from an angel's wing
　Seemed floating from the skies.

Then thick and fast, and faster still,
   In myriads they descend;
Well pleased, she marked their varied shapes
   In one white covering blend.

And Bessie thought, how beautiful
   Out in the storm to go,
And make deep footprints on the lawn,
   All in the lovely snow!

"In the old rocking-chair the nurse
   Is sleeping sound," said she,
"Her darning cotton round her neck,
   Her stockings on her knee.

"She will not hear me leave the room,
   And soon down-stairs I'll be!"
A minute more, and it was done,
   And little Bess was free.

All down the hidden lawn she ran,
   Although her shoes were thin;
Cold blew the piercing wintry blast—
   She didn't care a pin.

She jumped about, and tossed in air
   Great handfuls of the snow;
For nobody was near to say,
   "Oh, Bessie, don't do so!"

Then back again she lightly sped,
   And, at the kitchen door,
A poor, bareheaded man she saw,
   Who seemed to be fourscore.

His white hair on his shoulders flowed,
   Wet with the snow and sleet,
As there, with door ajar, he stood,
   Assistance to entreat.

The servants all at dinner sat,
   And ate the good roast beef;
They bade the poor old man "Begone!"
   And gave him no relief.

Then Bessie's heart felt nigh to break;
   Snug in her pocket lay
A rosy apple—it was all
   She had to give away.

This to the aged man she gave
   (Ah! 'twas a present cold),
But the warm tears ran down his cheeks,
   Her pity to behold.

And Bessie never will forget
   How, with those streaming eyes,
He blessed her with his trembling lips—
   No, never! till she dies.

THE BOY WHO WAS AFRAID OF THE DARK.

HERE was once a fine boy, his fond parents'
sole joy,
    Residing in Barnsbury Park ;
From a feeling of shame I can't mention his
name—
    For he was afraid of the dark !

When put into bed, for a truth it is said,
    He would tremble and cry with affright ;
And fall in a rage, although six years of age,
    If nurse was not by with a light.

One day as he sat playing games with the cat,
    His mother said, " Listen, my dear ;
Nurse stays with no light in your bedroom to-
night,
    For it's time you got over your fear.

" In your pretty white bed there is nothing to dread,
    With kind friends so near you below ;
So mind you don't pout, nor be cross, and cry out,
    For I seek but your good, you well know."

The little boy heard, but he spoke not a word,
    For a wicked thought came in his mind :
" My bedpost I'll scratch with a lucifer match,
    And light it, if so I'm inclined.

" The candlestick stands always near to my hands,
    On the large dressing-table close by ;
I sha'n't be to blame if I strike up a flame,
    For I can't lie in darkness—not I."

Old Betty, that night, as she put out the light,
    Declared he was " better than gold ! "
For he never once said, " Nurse, stay by my bed,"
    But let her do what she was told.

But oh ! by-and-bye rose a terrible cry,
    You'd never forget all your days !
Mamma she ran out, and beheld, without doubt,
    Her boy rushing down in a blaze.

She smothered him quite with a rug, in her fright,
    And rolled him about on the floor;
While, writhing with pain, he screamed once and again,
    " I'll never strike fire any more !

" I dropped a bright spark as I stood in the dark,
    And my night-dress that instant flamed high ;
I've done a bad thing, and I burn, smart, and sting,
    And where shall I go if I die ? "

He was carried to bed, and the doctor he said,
    He feared 'twas a very sad case;
For though well prepared to hope life might be spared,
    He dreaded deep scars on his face.

And day after day the young sufferer lay
    On his pillow, in sorrow and pain;
Till sweet Spring anew came with violets blue,
    But she brought not his beauty again.

His cheeks, scarred and pale, told so fearful a tale
    Of the dangers of dropping a spark,
That the children next door would have candles no more,
    But all went to bed in the dark.

"REMEMBER THE GUY!"

T was a Fifth of November eve,
    And down came the drizzling rain;
Yet the crackers banged, and the blue wheels
        whirled,
    And the serpents they hissed again.

Mamma on the sofa sat,
    Stitching for rosy Nell,
When a rustling she heard at the parlour door,
    What was it she could not tell.

Then two little girls rushed in,
    So merry and full of fun;
They scarce could stand on their round, fat legs,
    For the wonderful things they'd done!

Mamma would have hid her face—
    Such terrible masks they wore;
But they climbed her knees, and they held her hands,
    And shouted and laughed the more.

Then over the road they ran,
    To grandpa, who lived close by,
And burst in the room as he sipped his tea,
    With—"Please remember the Guy!"

Then grandpapa laughed, and tossed
  Some money high out of reach ;
And proudly the little girls ran home,
  Wealthy, with fourpence each.

Said Polly to rosy Nell,
  " What do you mean to buy ?
A pretty kaleidoscope I should like ;"
  Cried Nelly, " And so should I !

" Mamma, will you let us go
  To-morrow, if it is fair,
To spend our money at Mrs. Drum's,
  In the toy-shop near the square ? "

" Dears," said mamma, " pray don't
  Squander it all in toys ;
Would it not buy two loaves of bread
  For hungry girls and boys ? "

Then quiet was little Nell,
  And her thoughtful eyes grew bright ;
" I know what I'll do," she quickly said,
  And ran out with footstep light.

Mamma had a pretty box,
  On which it was written—" Please
Drop in a penny, if you can,
  For children over the seas.

"To poor little blacks afar
  Your money shall all be given;
Who never have heard a single word
  Of Jesus Christ or heaven.

" 'Twill buy them the Bible true,
  'Twill teach them to sing and pray;
So shall they rise, with beaming eyes,
  To bless you, the last great day."

Then into the box she dropped
  Two pennies, with cheerful smile;
But Polly, who followed her, stood behind,
  Grasping hers tight the while.

Which was the happiest child ?
  " Polly," perhaps you'd say,
Had you looked through the bright kaleidoscope
  She brought from the shop next day.

I think it was little Nell,
  Though all that her pence could get
Was merely a mimic cockchafer,
  On a wax leaf neatly set.

For something within her said,
  " 'Tis selfish ourselves to please;"
And a voice in her ear said, " Thank you, dear!"
  And it came from over the seas.

But grieved was her heart at night,
    To hear a most startling crash;
Poor Polly's toy from the drawers had rolled,
    And, oh! what a *dreadful* smash!

THE MUMMY WHEAT.

 EHOLD how pleasant to the eye
        Yon waving corn appears;
    The slender stalks swayed to and fro
        Beneath the golden ears.

Strange is the story of the seed
    That first was planted there,
How marvellous the withered grain
    A hundredfold should bear!

Within a silent tomb it passed
    A lapse of ages slow,
Bound in a dark Egyptian's hand
    Three thousand years ago.

Portrayed upon the massive walls
    Might all his deeds be viewed,
But none had ever yet disturbed
    The awful solitude.

At length within the sculptured cell
  A stranger dared to tread;
And lo! with sacrilegious hands
  He stole the ancient dead.

Yes! from the gorgeous sepulchre
  He bore him far away,
Till here on British ground he laid
  His venerable prey.

With careful fingers he removed
  The swathings one by one,
And gazed at last upon the form
  Of Egypt's swarthy son.

And straight arose the fragrant scent
  Of spices, oils, and balm;
And grains of corn went rolling down
  From off the blackened palm,

Grains that perchance were treasured up
  In Canaan's time of dearth;
Dry as they were, we planted them,
  In hope, beneath the earth.

The gentle rain of heaven came down,
  And soft, refreshing dew;
The mummy wheat their influence felt,
  Awoke to life, and grew!

G

And lo! the springing blades came forth
　　As tender, fresh, and green,
As though the parent grain last year
　　Within the ear had been.

And now the tall and fragile stem
　　Its graceful head uprears;
And see! within the bursting husk
　　The yellow corn appears.

Come hither, ye whose patient hands
　　" Beside all waters " sow;
The lovely crop ye long to view
　　In God's good time will grow.

In faith and hope a mother taught
　　Her lisping babe to pray;
The seed she planted in his heart
　　Sprang when his head was grey.

Go forth with courage, still your bread
　　" Upon the waters " cast;
Though vainly sought for many days,
　　It *shall* be found at last.

" I'M HERE."

HEN all its glory o'er the sea
　　October's sunshine threw,
And lighted up ten thousand waves
　　Upon its bosom blue,

A father and a joyous child
　　Unfurled the snowy sail,
And o'er the rippling waters sped
　　Before the gentle gale.

Loud laughed the happy boy, as soon
　　They neared a lovely isle;
"Oh, father, father, let me stay,
　　And wander there awhile!

" Strange seaweeds on the pebbly beach,
　　Fresh shells and flowers I see;—
Oh! leave me there—then onward sail,
　　And come again for me !"

The father, to the child's request,
　　A favouring answer gave,
And bade him watch his swift return
　　Across the dark blue wave.

Then forward rode the white-winged bark
    Upon the heaving main,
Still lessening, till a speck it seemed
    Upon the watery plain.

But suddenly the sky grew dark,
    The waves were bright no more;
As dense a mist as ever rose
    Hung over sea and shore.

The father thought upon his child,
    And hastened to return;
But of that lovely isle, alas!
    No trace could he discern.

Anxious and sad, and sore perplexed,
    He wandered here and there,
Till childish accents, clear and sweet,
    Rang through the murky air.

It was his darling's well-known voice,
    Exclaiming, "Father dear!
You cannot see me through the mist,
    But steer straight on—I'm here!"

The parent to his joyful heart
    Hath pressed his child once more;
And safely through the blinding fog
    Their bark has reached the shore.

But in a fortnight from that day,
   Tears, briny tears were shed;
"The mourners went about the streets"—
   The fair young boy was dead.

They laid the little lifeless form
   Beneath the verdant sod,
And thought upon that gentle soul
   Gone home to dwell with God.

But when that mourning parent stands
   Beside the tiny grave,
He hears those accents—silver sweet—
   Once heard across the wave.

From heaven above they seem to fall,—
   "Oh, father, father dear!
Earth's mists obscure me from thy sight,
   But steer straight on—I'm here!"

MARY GONE HOME.

EAR little Mary! Is she gone,
  The lovely child that once we knew?
With all her glossy, clustering curls,
  And thoughtful eyes of heavenly blue.

How lightly sprang her fairy feet
  To meet us, down the oaken stair!
While her gay laugh rang like a peal
  Of merry bells upon the air.

She was a child of beauty rare,
  Of truthful eye and modest grace;
All must remember her who once
  Looked on her fair and pleasant face.

Young as she was, she helped the poor,
  And cheered them in the daily strife;
And taught to many a youthful mind
  The solemn words of endless life.

Beloved by all (for *all* she loved)—
  Of home the light, of friends the pride—
Full many a bitter tear was shed,
  That village through, when Mary died.

It must have been a sad, sad time,
  Within the pastor's house that day,
When, to the rustic church close by,
  They bore dear Mary slow away.

And scalding tears fell down like rain,
  And deep sobs burst from many a breast,
When in the chancel old they laid
  All that remained of her to rest.

Their eyes were all so dim with grief,
  They could not see her as she stood
In glory at her Lord's right hand,
  Arrayed in garments washed in blood.

They could not see her as she knelt,
  And cast her crown before His feet;
While her triumphant welcome home
  Still echoed down the golden street.

Yet *there*, in radiant garb, she bent,
  Safe from the storm that swept below,
And there her glorious song shall rise,
  While countless ages onward flow.

THE WINDY NIGHT.

'WAS night, and by my parlour fire
　　I sat and worked alone,
And heard the wild March wind sweep by,
　　With howl, and shriek, and groan;
And great trees rocked, and chimneys crashed,
　　Before the hurrying blast,
And shattered fragments strewed the roads
　　With ruin as it passed.

While trembling at the tempest's force,
　　As, on that awful night,
It crushed the strongest works of man
　　With its tremendous might,—
The sweet tones of a childish voice
　　Came floating down the stairs,—
"I lay my griefs on Jesus,
　　My burdens and my cares."

That moment, from the loosened roof,
　　A mass of stonework fell!
Alarmed, I climbed the stairs, to know
　　My babes were safe and well;

That little voice was trilling yet
  Of trust in love divine,—
" I rest my soul on Jesus,
  This weary soul of mine."

Louder and louder roared the blast,
  Around, above, below ;
The very houses at its will
  Seemed rocking to and fro.
And in the pause of wind and storm,
  Still rose the childish song,—
" I long to be with Jesus,
  Amid the white-robed throng."

Oh, when the final hurricane
  Shall sweep a sinking world,
And temple grand and towering steep
  In flaming gulfs are hurled !
Dear child ! may thy sweet confidence
  To our faint souls be given,
So shall our songs, amid the storm,
  Proclaim the peace of heaven.

THE ANGEL'S WHISPER.

THOU smil'st in thy sleep, my child;
  Is a white-robed angel near,
Telling sweet tales of the far-off land
  Into thy listening ear?

Hath he come on his sounding wings,
  To speak to my darling girl
Of the glorious city, with jasper walls,
  And radiant gates of pearl?

Perhaps, in a blessed dream,
  He taketh thee by the hand,
And leadeth thee down the golden streets
  Of the lovely and pleasant land.

And thou gazest on tearless eyes,
  Which sorrow may never dim,
And hearest with joy the ceaseless cry
  Of the kneeling seraphim.

It may be thy tiny feet
  Now stand on the crystal sea,
And thy stammering tongue is loosed to join
  In heaven's high harmony.

Seest thou the shining bands,
   Walking in spotless white,
Striking their glorious harps of gold
   In the great Eternal's sight ?

Softly the vision flies !
   Gently the lids unclose !
Still on the wintry plain of earth
   Bloometh my fresh young rose !

God give thee grace, my child,
   To realize things that seem,
And prove, at the close of life, that heaven
   Is more than a mother's dream.

THE RAINY DAY;

OR, EMILY'S FAITH.

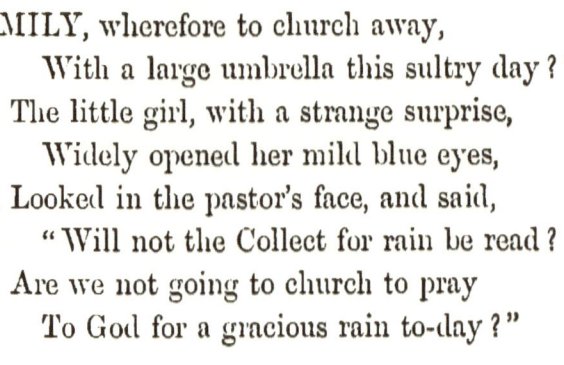

MILY, wherefore to church away,
    With a large umbrella this sultry day?"
The little girl, with a strange surprise,
    Widely opened her mild blue eyes,
Looked in the pastor's face, and said,
    "Will not the Collect for rain be read?
Are we not going to church to pray
    To God for a gracious rain to-day?"

Sadly the worthy pastor smiled,
    And blessed the faith of the guileless child;
Sadly he smiled, for a thought of grief
    Stole o'er his heart at his unbelief;
And the prayer that went up to his Lord above
    Was, "Oh for such trustful faith and love!"

Within the walls of their ancient fane
    The worshippers knelt—and they prayed for rain;
No breath through the open windows there
    Fluttered a leaf as they bowed in prayer;
And the cloudless heaven, it seemed to say,
    "Vainly ye supplicate rain to-day."

Now, from the oaken pulpit old,
    A tale of Elijah's faith was told;
But the pastor paused, for a sudden breeze
    Woke the still landscape and rocked the trees,
Swung the worn casements to and fro,
    Played in the leaves of the books below;
And the peal of the distant thunder roared,—
    "Surely there's nothing too hard for the Lord!"

Again he told of the "little cloud"
    Shading the heavens in darkening shroud;
The bright sky faded the while he spoke,
    Nearer and nearer the thunder broke;
And, strangely welcome, the gladdening rain
    Pattered and clattered on roof and pane.

The blessing given, the service o'er,
    A waiting crowd throngs the old church door
Tears are in Emily's eyes of blue,
    Vainly she strives for a passage through;—
Soon does the pastor her grief allay,
    He takes her hand, and they make him way.

He tells of her faith to the standers by—
    Her large umbrella he holds on high;
She begs him its friendly shelter share,
    With modest curtsey and gentle air;
And proudly happy she leads away
    Her pastor homewards that rainy day.

LIZZIE.

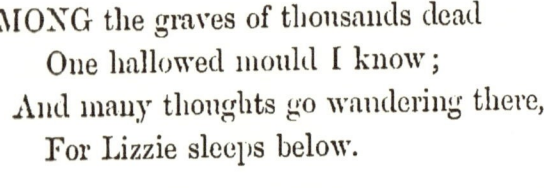

'MONG the graves of thousands dead
    One hallowed mould I know;
And many thoughts go wandering there,
    For Lizzie sleeps below.

Lizzie, a happy, radiant beam
    Of blessed sunshine, given
To stream athwart our path awhile,
    Then vanish back to heaven.

She was a fair and smiling babe,
    So gentle to behold;
It seemed as if a little lamb
    Had strayed from heaven's fold.

And she would raise her sweet blue eyes,
    And sigh when worn with pain,
As if she wished her Shepherd dear
    Would fetch her home again.

For death's rude storm came sweeping o'er
    Our blossom of the May;
And like a fair and drooping flower
    She faded day by day.

We watched her when the blushing east
　　Proclaimed the morning nigh,
We watched her when the quiet stars
　　By thousands thronged the sky;

And many a night and many a morn
　　Still found us watching there,
Before the dreary death-shade fell
　　Upon her forehead fair.

It came at last, that time of gloom!
　　We knew her hour was come;
Her small white feet already pressed
　　The threshold of her home.

And a sweet voice went murmuring round
　　From One we might not see;
"Suffer the little child," it said,
　　"To come and dwell with Me!"

She never felt the winter's frost,
　　Nor heard its wild winds blow;
Safe in the arms of God she lay,
　　Before the fall of snow.

Ah! swiftly from its fragile cage
　　Our pretty bird took wing;
It fluttered through the loosened wires,
　　And soared to heaven to sing.

And from the everlasting hills
  Sweet strains came floating down;
All heaven was glad—a new, soft pearl
  Adorned the Savour's crown.

White is the world's tempestuous sea
  With the rough billows' foam;
But the first wave that lashed her bark
  Was that which washed it home.

J. & W. RIDER, Printers, London.